This book is presented to the

Sun Valley School Library

in honor of

Delia Farrell

grade Kdgn   year 1993

Annabel

by Janice Boland
pictures by Megan Halsey

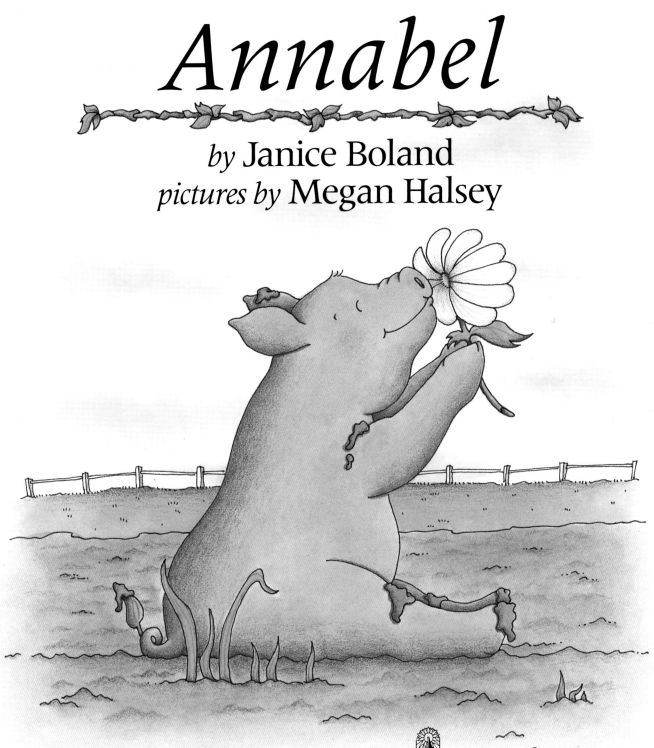

Dial Books for Young Readers 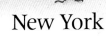 New York

Published by Dial Books for Young Readers
A Division of Penguin Books USA Inc.
375 Hudson Street
New York, New York 10014

Printed in Hong Kong
by South China Printing Company (1988) Limited
First Edition
1 3 5 7 9 10 8 6 4 2

Library of Congress Cataloging in Publication Data
Boland, Janice.
Annabel / by Janice Boland ; pictures by Megan Halsey—1st ed.
p.   cm.
Summary: A little pig with a desire to be important and
do something wonderful ventures off to ask a horse, dog, and hen
why each of them is unique.
ISBN 0-8037-1254-5.—ISBN 0-8037-1255-3 (lib. bdg.)
[1. Individuality—Fiction. 2. Animals—Fiction.]
I. Halsey, Megan, ill. II. Title.
PZ7.B635849An 1993   [E]—dc20   91-46490   CIP   AC

The full-color artwork was prepared using pen and ink, watercolor, dyes,
and colored pencils. It was then scanner-separated and reproduced as red,
blue, yellow, and black halftones.

To my mother and for Jim, who made it possible
J. B.

For my wonderful sister, Jodi
M. H.

Annabel rolled over in the mud puddle. She looked up at the sky. It was so blue.

"I don't want to be a little pig today, Mama," she said. "I want to be big. I want to be important. I want to do something wonderful!" she cried as she whirled on her toes.

"Of course you do, dear," said Mother Pig, snuggling deeper into the mud. "Just be yourself," she called as Annabel skipped out of sight.

Annabel skidded into a horse. She looked way, way up at him, and said, "You look like you do something big around here."

"I certainly do," neigh, neigh, neighed the horse. "I plow the field."

"Oh, that *is* big!" said Annabel. "I will do it too!"

She hitched herself to the plow and walked beside the horse. Together they plowed the field. This way and that way, back and forth, around and around they went.

When they were finished, the field was a patchwork of zigzags, stripes, and squares.

"Wow!" whinnied the horse. "I could never have done that without you! You can do big things too, Annabel."

"I knew it!" cried Annabel, and away she bounced.

Annabel bumped into a dog. "Are you important?" Annabel asked.

"I am very important," woof, woof, woofed the dog. "I guard the field and the farm."

"That *is* important!" said Annabel. "I will do it too!"

"Shh, shh, shhhh," whispered the dog. "I hear crooks and robbers and thieves."

He growled.

He howled.

Annabel grunted.

She squealed.

She oink, oink, oinked, and all the foxes, the wolves, the raccoons, and the weasels fled to their dens in the woods.

"I could never have done that without you. You are important too, Annabel," said the dog.

"I know," said Annabel, and away she pranced.

Annabel met a red-feathered hen. "Are you doing something wonderful?" she asked.

"Yes," cluck, cluck, clucked the hen. "I'm keeping my eggs warm."

"That *is* wonderful!" said Annabel. "I will do it too!"

She wiggled into the nest with the hen. Together they sat on the eggs. The eggs grew warmer and warmer. CRACK! They started to hatch.

Soon the nest was filled with peeping yellow chicks.
"How lovely," crooned the hen. "You are wonderful, Annabel."
"Yes, I am," said Annabel.

Annabel danced a jig.
She was big.
She was important.
She was wonderful!
"I can't wait to tell Mama!" she cried.

On the way home Annabel stopped at the pond for a cool drink of water.

She looked down.

"Oh, no!" she gasped.

In the water she saw the same little eyes and ears, and the same little snout.

Annabel ran all the way home.

"Oh, Mama," she wailed. "I'm still a little pig. I'm just me."
"That's wonderful, dear," said Mother Pig.
"It is?" squealed Annabel.

"Yes," said Mother Pig. "It is absolutely wonderful!"